MY FAVORITE DOG

GOLDEN RETRIEVERS

by K.C. Kelley

Dog Expert: Beth Adelman, MS

Former editor, *American Kennel Club Gazette*

Kaleidoscope

Minneapolis, MN

BIGFOOT BOOKS

The Quest for Discovery Never Ends

This edition first published in 2021 by Kaleidoscope Publishing, Inc.

No part of this publication may be reproduced in whole or in part without written permission of the publisher.

For information regarding permission, write to Kaleidoscope Publishing, Inc.
6012 Blue Circle Drive
Minnetonka, MN 55343

Library of Congress Control Number
2020936274

ISBN
978-1-64519-442-2 (library bound)
978-1-64519-454-5 (ebook)

FIND ME
IF YOU CAN!

Bigfoot lurks within one of the images in this book. It's up to you to find him!

TABLE OF
CONTENTS

Here Comes a Golden Retriever!

Katie stared out her front window. She was so excited! Her new dog was coming home today. Katie wanted a friendly dog. She wanted a dog who was not too big, but not too small.

Her parents had gone to an animal shelter. Katie's new dog would be a **rescue dog**. She would make sure her pet had a great home.

She already had the name picked out. Katie's new dog would be called Angel! Where would Angel sleep? What would she eat? Would she learn tricks? Katie had so many questions.

A car stopped in front. Katie's questions vanished.

"Look!" she yelled. "It's a Golden Retriever!"

Chapter 1
The Story of Golden Retrievers

Golden Retrievers like Angel are originally from Scotland. Dudley Marjoribanks was the Scottish Lord Tweedmouth. He owned a huge **estate**. He loved to

FUN FACT

The American Kennel Club keeps track of dog breeds. The AKC first registered Goldens in 1925.

hunt. In 1868, he began mixing breeds of dogs. The result was the Golden Retriever.

Lord Tweedmouth's dogs were strong and full of energy. They loved to run in the woods. They were also great swimmers. They helped him when he hunted. The Goldens would retrieve, or pick up, animals that Lord Tweedmouth caught.

Goldens came to America in the early 1900s. Today, they are one of the most popular breeds!

This gathering of Goldens was held at Lord Tweedmouth's old estate in Scotland.

HELPING OUT

Golden Retrievers can be trained to help people. Some Goldens work as guide dogs. They help blind people move around safely. Goldens can also work in search and rescue.

Dog breeds are put into groups. Goldens are in the Sporting Group. The name comes from the dogs' first jobs. They helped "sportsmen" in the fields. Other dogs in the Sporting Group are Pointers, Setters, and Spaniels. All were bred to help people hunt for food.

Angel doesn't hunt. But she still needs to be active. Katie makes sure to play with Angel every day. She throws a ball for Angel or goes for a run. Staying active keeps Angel healthy.

Katie also takes Angel to the water whenever she can. Golden Retrievers *love* to swim. Katie loves to watch Angel shake her fur to dry off!

Katie's friend has an older Golden named Gordo. Gordo is almost as active as Angel. He's not a puppy anymore, but he acts like one! That's not surprising for a Golden Retriever.

Golden Retrievers are very smart, too. They can be trained easily. Katie thinks Angel always seems to be having a good time, even when she's learning.

FUN FACT
President Gerald Ford had a Golden named Liberty. She lived at the White House!

WHERE GOLDEN RETRIEVERS COME FROM

Guisachan, Scotland

NORWAY

SCOTLAND

North Sea

IRELAND

ENGLAND

GERMANY

FRANCE

Atlantic Ocean

SPAIN

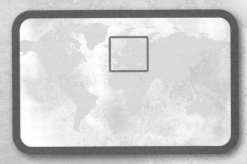

Chapter 2

Looking at a Golden Retriever

Katie loves combing Angel's hair. It is so thick and shiny. The beautiful golden color gives the breed its name. Golden Retrievers can actually be several colors, including golden, of course. You might see one that is light red. Others are light yellow. Some are almost white.

Goldens have fluffy tails. Katie watches Angel's tail wag. When Angel is worried, her tail might droop. But that's not very often. Angel is a very happy dog!

Angel has dark brown eyes, like all Goldens. They have black noses, too.

THE
GOLDEN
RETRIEVER

MALES

HEIGHT*:
23–24 inches (58–61 cm)

WEIGHT:
65–75 lbs. (29.4–34 kg)

FEMALES

HEIGHT*:
21.5–22.5 inches (54–57 cm)

WEIGHT:
55–65 lbs. (25–29.4 kg)

The height of a dog is measured from the top of the shoulder, not from the top of the head.

TAIL
Carried down or level with the back

LEGS
Strong and muscular

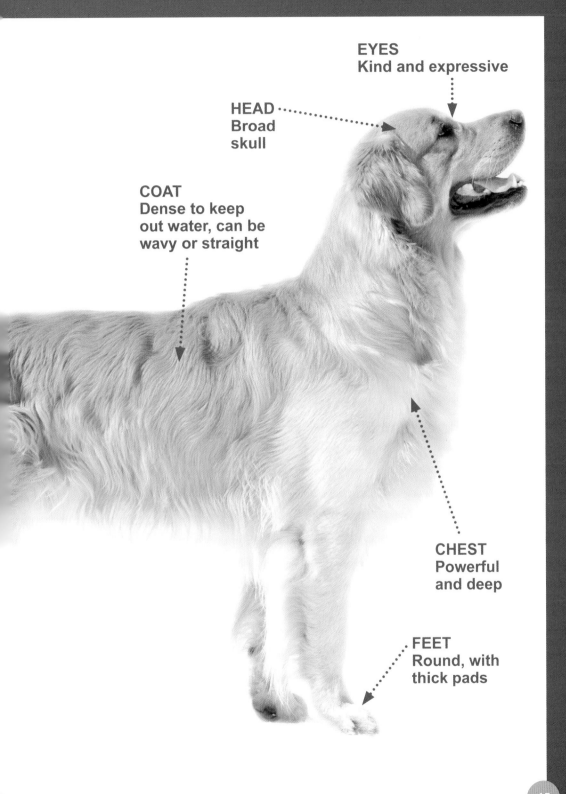

EYES
Kind and expressive

HEAD
Broad
skull

COAT
Dense to keep
out water, can be
wavy or straight

CHEST
Powerful
and deep

FEET
Round, with
thick pads

Handlers work with dogs at shows.

At dog shows, experts look at each dog and compare them to a breed standard. That's a description of what a perfect dog should look like. Golden Retrievers are fun to watch at dog shows. They bounce around the show ring. Their fluffy tails are wagging. Goldens compete first in the Sporting Group. Then they have a chance to win Best in Show.

The most famous U.S. show is the Westminster Kennel Club Show. It is held in New York City. Strangely, a Golden has never won Best in Show there.

Katie doesn't care about awards. Angel is her best dog every day!

Chapter 3
Meet a Golden Retriever!

Katie takes Angel for a walk. Katie watches Angel's bouncy **stride**. Goldens love to move and run, and it shows. When she's not sniffing the ground, Angel has her head up. She looks around eagerly. Her eyes are alert and shining. She almost looks like she's smiling!

Walking Angel is important. Golden Retrievers have a lot of energy to burn.

In 2013, a Golden set a record for the world's loudest bark! Charlie's bark was louder than a chainsaw!

Katie teaches Angel how to walk on a leash. Angel learns not to pull away. Katie and Angel make a great team.

As they walk, Katie sees other people smile at them. Goldens make people happy! They are very friendly dogs. They love to play with other dogs and meet new people.

Katie loves spending time with Angel. It's like having a furry friend!

PUPPY TIME!

When Angel was a puppy, she was super cute! Golden Retriever puppies need lots of care. They are very active. They love to chew everything. Make sure your home is ready for a puppy if you get a Golden.

Katie is happy she lives in a house with a yard. She knows that Angel needs lots of places to play. Angel would not be as happy in a small apartment.

Katie and her parents studied before they got Angel. They made sure their home was the right one. All dog partners need to know about their new dogs.

Chapter 4

Caring for a Golden Retriever

It's bath time. Katie has to help Angel stay healthy. Giving her a bath is one way to do that. Goldens have a lot of hair. Keeping it clean can be hard work. Angel can get very muddy!

Katie gives Angel a bath using warm water. She uses dog shampoo. Then she rinses off the shampoo. Katie uses a towel, but Angel is good at drying herself!

After Angel is dry, Katie brushes her hair again.

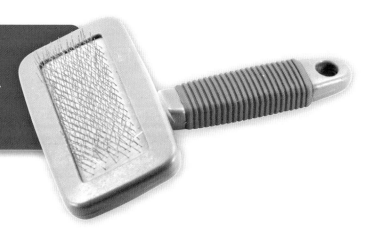

A good tool to use on a Golden is called a slicker brush. It has soft metal teeth.

A big tub can make dog baths easier.

After the bath, it's time to eat. Katie makes sure Angel eats the right kind of dog food. Katie and her mom took Angel to the veterinarian. They learned that Angel should eat twice a day. The vet chose a food that had the meat and nutrition Angel needs.

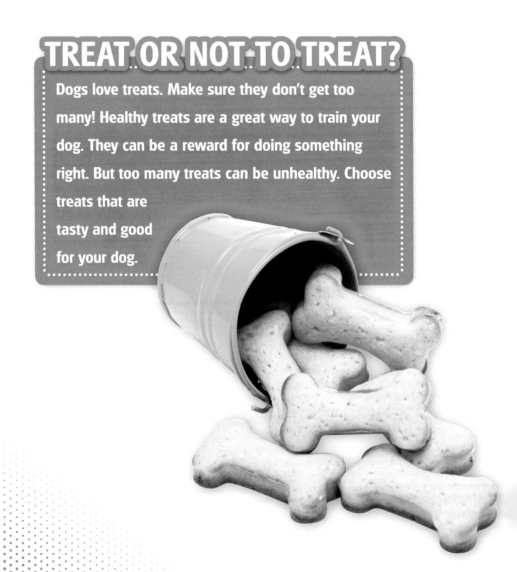

TREAT OR NOT TO TREAT?

Dogs love treats. Make sure they don't get too many! Healthy treats are a great way to train your dog. They can be a reward for doing something right. But too many treats can be unhealthy. Choose treats that are tasty and good for your dog.

After she eats, Angel's teeth need cleaning, just like yours. Katie tells Angel to sit. Then she carefully holds Angel's jaw and brushes her teeth. It took Katie a while to get Angel to like this. Now they work together like a teeth-cleaning team!

Katie and Angel have had a great day together. Katie is so happy that Angel came to live with them. Golden Retrievers are popular dogs for good reasons, Katie thinks.

It's bed time. Katie makes sure Angel went out to the yard one more time. After Angel came in, Katie made sure she had water for the night. Now, Katie sends Angel off to her own bed.

In the morning, it will be time to eat another good meal—and then play all day!

FUN FACT

A Golden named Buddy was the star of a series of movies called *Air Bud*.

THE BOOK

After reading the book, it's time to think about what you learned.
Try the following exercises to jumpstart your ideas.

RESEARCH

FIND OUT MORE. There is so much more to find out about Golden Retrievers. Visit the American Kennel Club's site to research Goldens. Or look for a Golden Retriever Club in your area. You can meet other people who love your favorite breed!

CREATE

TIME FOR ART. Many types of dogs are mascots for sports teams. Pick your favorite dog breed and design a new logo for a sports team named for that dog. What colors will you use? What sort of lettering? Will the dog look friendly or fierce? Look at other dog mascot logos for inspiration.

DISCOVER

LOTS OF BREEDS. This book is about your favorite dog breed. But there are hundreds more around the world. Visit the AKC site or those of other dog organizations. What other breeds can you discover? Which breeds are related to your favorite? What is the most interesting new breed you have discovered?

GROW

HELP OUT! Animal shelters can be great places to volunteer. Contact a shelter near you and find out if you can help. Or can your family donate food or gear to help rescue dogs? Find out why dogs end up in shelters. Is there anything you can do to help them find homes?

RESEARCH NINJA

Visit *www.ninjaresearcher.com/4422* to learn how
to take your research skills and book report writing to the next level!

RESEARCH ·····································

DIGITAL LITERACY TOOLS

SEARCH LIKE A PRO
Learn about how to use search engines to find useful websites.

FACT OR FAKE?
Discover how you can tell a trusted website from an untrustworthy resource.

TEXT DETECTIVE
Explore how to zero in on the information you need most.

SHOW YOUR WORK
Research responsibly—learn how to cite sources.

WRITE ·····································

GET TO THE POINT
Learn how to express your main ideas.

PLAN OF ATTACK
Learn prewriting exercises and create an outline.

DOWNLOADABLE REPORT FORMS

Further Resources

BOOKS

Aboff, Marcie. *Fast Facts About Golden Retrievers.* Mankato, MN: Pebble Books, 2020.

Miles, Ellen. *Goldie (The Puppy Place).* New York: Scholastic, 2006.

Stevens, Janet. *My Big Dog.* New York: Dragonfly Books, 2009.

WEBSITES

FACTSURFER

Factsurfer.com gives you a safe, fun way to find more information.

1. Go to www.factsurfer.com.

2. Enter "Golden Retrievers" into the search box and click 🔍

3. Select your book cover to see a list of related websites.

Glossary

estate: a large piece of land surrounding a big house.

nutrition: getting the right kind of food to be healthy.

rescue dog: a dog who has been brought home from an animal shelter by a new owner.

retrieve: pick up and bring something to someone.

search and rescue: dogs who find people after a disaster.

stride: how an animal or a person walks.

veterinarian: a doctor for animals.

Index

PHOTO CREDITS

About the Author

K.C. Kelley is the author of more than 200 nonfiction books for kids. He has written about sports, science, nature, history, and more. He lives with Shadow, a mixed-breed dog who barks too much!